Good Mornin', Ms. America

The U.S.A. in Verse

By J. Patrick Lewis

Illustrated by Mark Clapsadle

GINGHAM DOG PRESS

Columbus, Ohio

For Sanay,

"beautiful like the moon"

With love,

Grandpat

To my brother, Tom, and sister, Judy

Mark

School Specialty Publishing

Text © 2007 J. Patrick Lewis. Art © 2007 School Specialty Publishing.
Published by Gingham Dog Press, an imprint of School Specialty Publishing, a member of the School Specialty Family.

Library of Congress Cataloging-in-Publication Data is on file with the publisher.

Send all inquiries to:
School Specialty Publishing
8720 Orion Place
Columbus, OH 43240-2111

ISBN 0-7696-3170-3

1 2 3 4 5 6 7 8 9 10 PHXBK 10 09 08 07 06

HaikUSA

To find out which state
has the longest coastline, as
usual, **ask a** kid.

If you visit us,
don't **miss our** incredible
gateway to the west!

"I'm **hating snow**, Dad!"
"It's **thawing, son**." (Anagrams
for a corner state.)

Together at the
beginning, apart at the
end: **connect I cut**.

Louisiana:
Only state with USA
hidden within it.

Behead and curtail
the word **foregon**e, and you end
up with _____.

I am rounded at
the ends, but in the middle,
I am almost high.

Oh, Rocky Mountain
cool road: anagram for me
at my highest peak.

Look to me for the
most Native Americans.
An arid zone, I.

I am the only
miss whose sis sits in the midst
of a state like this.

The most rural state.
Official drink: milk. I am
a tad north, OK?

Unscramble **Hawaiian**
for a two-week vacation.
Ahaa, I win!

USA in Short
The State Initials Game

No **MA**tter where you **AR**,
RIght here **OR** fara**WA**,
If you **CA**n na**ME** the states
(**AZ** in the USA),

So**ME**o**NE** **MI**ght **NV** you!
TAKe a**NY** state there is,
Abbrev**IA**te it, k**ID**,
AND you **CO**uld **WI**n t**HI**s quiz!

So p**UT** your bra**IN** **CA**p on.
Get pe**NCIL**s ready…Go!
It's the state **IN**iti**AL**s **GAME**.
Di**SC**over **MANY MO**!

Spellbound A-M-E-R-I-C-A

If windy's where you want to go,
Try C-H-I-_-_-_-O.

If sticky's what you'd like to try,
Then fly to M-I-A-_-_.

If rainy's where you'd like to be,
Try S-_-_-T-T-L-E.

Baked beans, Red Sox, and Irishmen
Means you're in B-_-_-T-O-N.

Where'd you find high heat index?
In P-H-O-E-N-_-_.

Sunny, smoggy? Can you guess?
Los A-N-G-E-_-_-S!

Monumental Riddles

You'll love the view.
You'll love the guide.
You may not love
The donkey ride!
...
Goodbye, caution!
Hello, peril!
Everybody,
Grab your barrel!
...
Huckleberry Finn
Invites you in
For mischief
Subterranean.
...
Wind and rain
Cannot erase us:
Four presi-dental
Happy faces.

Surprise! I am
The rising geyser:
Earth's most famous
Vaporizer.
...
I'm the waterway
Of the Delta Queens
From Minnesota
To New Orleans.
...
Every 23 seconds,
Planes take off from there:
Oh, wind! Oh, sky!
Oh, air!

Slowly Around the USA

If I had nothing else to do,
I'd write a birthday card to you.

I'd send it off to someone who,
Say, lived in Millinocket, Maine,
And very carefully explain
That he should quickly mail it on
By way of Portland, Oregon.

And when it got there, they would know
To forward it to Buffalo,
New York, so that the person there
Would have to send it first-class air
To Boston, Mass., and back again
By overnight delivery.

Then, from Nashville, Tennessee, to Knox-
Ville, care of Auntie's P.O. Box,
So she could zip it by express
To your Chicago, Ill., address.

And someday, maybe mid-July,
A birthday card! You'd wonder why
It took so long to get to you.
I'd call you up and tell you, too,
If I had nothing else to do.

America on the Moon

Two high fliers, Buzz and Neil,
Said they couldn't wait to feel
Just what kind of moon it was.
"Take a look around," said Buzz.

Open the hatch and out the door,
Down the ladder to the moonlit floor.
After he had sunk his heel
Into the dusty ocean, Neil
Knew what a lovely moon it was.
"One small step…" said Neil to Buzz.

What is a Midwestern Farm?

A field where they allow
cow,

Where mice enjoy a hay
day,

Where you can see sweet corn
born,

Where butterflies pursue
dew,

Where hog and sow and runt
grunt,

Where roosters turn the dawn
on.

Edgar Springs, Missouri?

(Center of the US Population)

Smack-de-do-dab in the middle
Of America's a little
Hamlet by the name of Edgar Springs.

And I think I oughta mention
(Could I have y'all's attention?)
'Cause it may not have the most familiar ring:

Hundred ninety (population),
Belly button of the nation,
One P.O.,
A general store,
A stop for gas.

It's a breadbox of a borough,
And the bloomin' Census Bureau
can't locate it with a magnifying glass!

The Bend in Bend, Oregon

If a limousine chauffeur
Goes around the bend in Bend,
Oregon, what could occur
Is that Bend would never end.

Going round and round, you see,
Never knowing where the end
Of the bend to Bend could be.
Here's what I would recommend:

Do not hire a chauffeur,
Even if he is your friend.
In the endless circle tour,
There's no end of bend to Bend!

Cincinnati Jump Rope Rhyme

Down in Cincinnati,
Seven **girls** skipped **school**,
Jumpin' through a **rib**bon,
Thinkin' **This** is so **cool**!

Rockin' to the **rhythm**,
All the **girls** wanna **go**
Down to Cincin**nati**-ati,
O-hi-**o**,
Down to Cincin**nati**-ati,
O-hi-o!

Good Mornin', Ms. America!

Good mornin', Mrs. Iowa!
How are you getting on?
Your corn is high, and my-oh-my,
Your wheat's a golden dawn.

How do you do, Miss New York City,
Standing in the shade
Of skyscrapers to see your
Famous ticker tape parade.

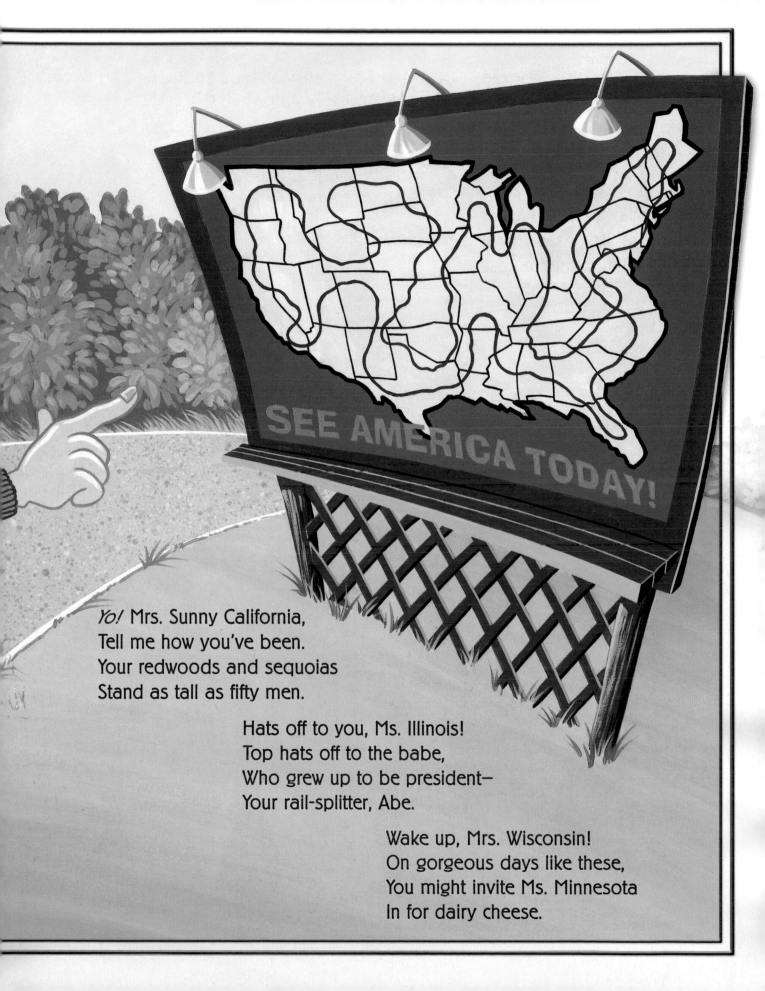

Yo! Mrs. Sunny California,
Tell me how you've been.
Your redwoods and sequoias
Stand as tall as fifty men.

Hats off to you, Ms. Illinois!
Top hats off to the babe,
Who grew up to be president—
Your rail-splitter, Abe.

Wake up, Mrs. Wisconsin!
On gorgeous days like these,
You might invite Ms. Minnesota
In for dairy cheese.

Hullo, Ms. Rose of Texas!
Well, how y'all, my dear?
Rollin' with the tumbleweed
And Texas longhorn steer?

¡Buenos Días, Ms. New Mexico!
Nevada, Arizona, West
Virginia, Arkansas…now see
If you can name the rest.

To Fifty Stately Daughters—
Each with a starring role—
Your mountains, rivers, steeples,
So many different peoples
Have made a nation whole,
Have made a nation whole.

The Appalachian Trail

Where the Appalachian Trail runs
From Georgia up to Maine
Two thousand crooked miles
Down a Million Story Lane,
Where the Appalachian Trail leaves
Rough history in its wake,
Two thousand star-dark miles
Celebrate their famed namesake,
A drama's playing out under
The ceiling of the fog—

A toad sits, apprehensive,
Musing on her travel log.

July 4th

Summer is a raspberry girl
On a simmer-down day
Hitting a T-ball over
A Dreamsicle truck,
Two window washers,
A Fourth-of-July flag,
Flying
All the way ooooooover
The man in the Moon-
Beam Dairy billboard,
And telling the super,
"That was sooooo easy."

Down Along the Illinois Line

Illinois Central
Comes a-rollin' down the tracks!
Conductor man's a-tossin'
Out the late mail sacks.

"First stop–Arcola!"
Clang-Clang the bells.

"Second stop–Tuscola!"
Conductor man yells.

Last stop–Pepsi-cola
On this mail train?

"Nope," says conductor man,
"Next–Champaign!"

House for Sale

Iona Big Sandy Surfside Home:
Brick, Gas, Big Chimney,
Telephone, Frostproof Amana,
Bath Addition.
Uno, Ware Igo,
Nothing Drab, Boring.
Udall Grow Happy, Carefree!

Why?

Cool Little Heaven Between
Simplicity, Romance.
Welcome, Paradise.
Fear Not.
Last Chance!

Friendly, Smiley?

Ubet, Junior!

Okay, Whynot?!

Dunmovin?
Hopeulikit.

NEW HIGH TECH TOOLS LOCATE BURROW!

EXCLUSIVE: Where the groundhog is hiding!

THE LOCAL
PENN CRIER

PUNXSUTAWNEY PHIL

At Gobbler's Knob, in Pennsylvane,
Groundhog says snow, and folks complain.

Groundhog says winter's gone for good-
They jump around the robin-hood!

On 2/2, Famous Forecast Phil
Unburrows from the side of the hill.

And if his shadow should appear?
There's six more weeks of winter here.

And if no shadow? Whadya know?
Last of the Punxsutawney snow!

But folks get colder by degrees,
'Cause nine times out of ten Phil sees

A groundhog shadow standing there
In very short long underwear.

WEATHER expert refuses to testify

Phil's case frozen!

PLUS: never-before-seen photos exclusively from Critter Cam!

Postcard from the San Diego Zoo

Look up *Wow!* in the dictionary.
This is what you'll find:
the hippopotamus in front
and my behind behind!

Florida

Orlando, Jacksonville, Miami—the Sunshine
State of Uncle Sammy—is home to 'gators,
crocodiles, flamingoes, hurricanes, and miles
of sunburned bathers; palm trees,
pelicans and ports; embarrassing
Bermuda shorts. On this map, you stick a
pin—here's where the Everglades begin.
Then like an army, they appear—TOURISTS!—
here,

here,

here,

and here!

Blues in Central Park

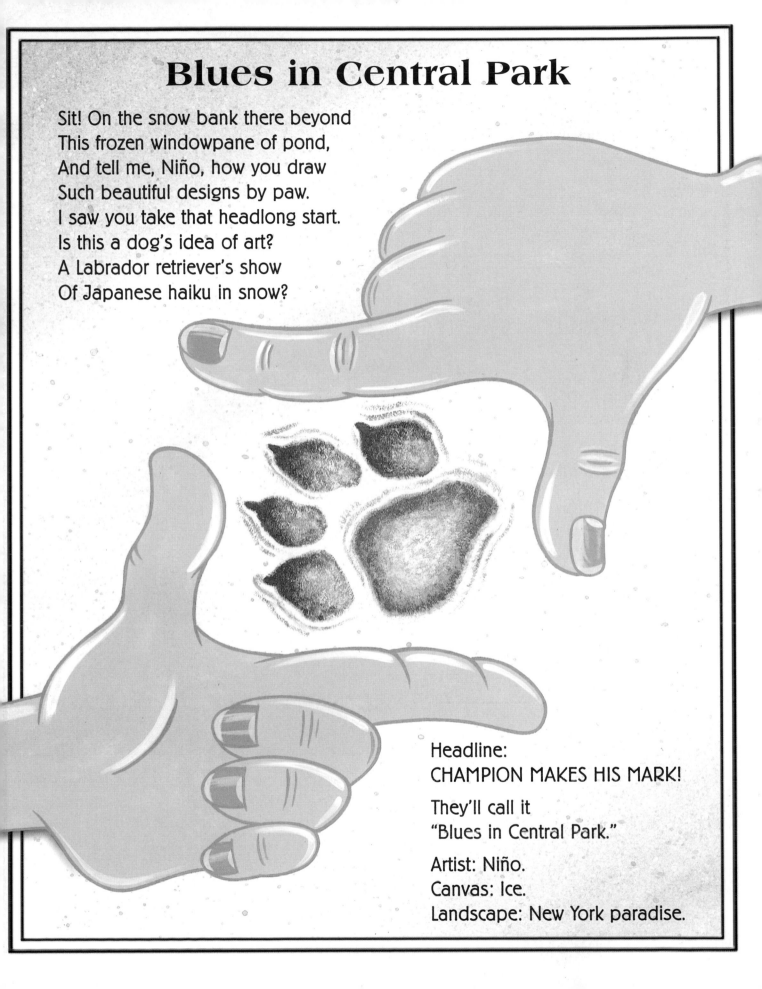

Sit! On the snow bank there beyond
This frozen windowpane of pond,
And tell me, Niño, how you draw
Such beautiful designs by paw.
I saw you take that headlong start.
Is this a dog's idea of art?
A Labrador retriever's show
Of Japanese haiku in snow?

Headline:
CHAMPION MAKES HIS MARK!

They'll call it
"Blues in Central Park."

Artist: Niño.
Canvas: Ice.
Landscape: New York paradise.

The Statue of Liberty (Afloat!)

What if the earth got hotter
And glaciers turned to water?
    Miss Liberty
    Would surely be
Our underwater daughter.

Her torch would still be showing
And she would be tiptoeing!
    Her guests would pour
    From every shore,
But they would all be rowing!

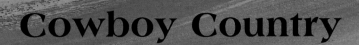

Cowboy Country

Red buries brown—autumn.

Red marries yellow—sunset.

Red rides west—sundown.

Red hides soil—dust.

Red burns orange—embers.

Red turns gray—ashes.

Red goes gold—evening.

Red grows old—rust.

A Mapmaker Draws America

First, I take a pointy pencil,
Ruler, protractor, and stencil.
   And I pick a likely spot
For a mountain, state park, freeway,
Island, reservoir, or seaway.
(I'm just kidding, Buster, we weigh
   All the evidence we've got.)

But I can't decide the color!
Lighter, brighter? Darker, duller?
   Paintbrush, watercolors, ink?
"Orange and purple for Nebraska?!"
"Why not blue and pink Alaska?!"
(So for highway maps, I ask a
   Kid, "Which color do you think?")

Did You Know?

Each word in the poem "House for Sale" is the name of a U.S. city.

Amana, IA
Bath Addition, PA
Between, GA
Big Chimney, WV
Big Sandy, WY
Boring, MD
Boring, OR
Brick, NJ
Carefree, AZ
Carefree, IN
Cool, CA
Drab, PA
Dunmovin, CA
Fear Not, PA
Friendly, WV
Frostproof, FL
Gas, KS
Grow, TX
Happy, TX
Home, OH
Home, PA
Hopeulikit, GA
Igo, CA
Iona, FL
Junior, WV
Last Chance, CA
Last Chance, CO
Little Heaven, DE

Nothing, AZ
Okay, AR
Okay, OK
Paradise, MI
Paradise, UT
Romance, MO
Simplicity, VA
Smiley, TX
Surfside, CA
Telephone, TX
Ubet, CA
Ubet, WI
Udall, KS
Uno, KY
Uno, PA
Ware, MA
Welcome, NC
Welcome, SC
Why, AZ
Whynot, NC

The U.S. bought Alaska from Russia for two cents an acre. Juneau that?

One vowel is repeated four times in Tennessee and Mississippi. Yiiiippppeeee!

More than any other U.S. state, Michigan has registered bowlers. To spare.

•••••

There are more moo-cows than people in Vermont. Many moo.

There are more sheep than people in Wyoming. Roaming.